This book
belongs to:

With thanks to my husband and my mom.

For Logan, who delights in the beauty of
even the smallest wonders.

"Let all that you do be done in love."
(1 Corinthians 16:14, ESV)
-M.R.E

To my wonderful wife for your
constant love and faith in me.

-K.R

The Legend of Dust Bunnies, a Fairy's Tale
© 2014 Michelle R. Eastman
All rights reserved.

ISBN: 978-0-9916244-7-8
Library of Congress Control Number: 2014904443

Byway Press, USA

The Legend of Dust Bunnies
a fairy's tale

Written by
Michelle R. Eastman
and illustrated by
Kevin Richter

The Legend of Dust Bunnies
began long ago,
in a house just like this one,
and here's how it goes...

First, you must know
what happens each night.
Asleep in our beds,
we don't see the sight.

Fairies spread dust
to the left and to the right.

The fairies proceed
at an uncanny pace,

and dirty our homes
with precision and grace.

The naughtiest nymphs,
along with their kin,
hold crumb-spitting contests
to see who will win.

With soot-loaded slingshots
pulled tight to their chests,
the husky, young fairies
make a terrible mess.

The daintiest ones
softly land on the drapes,
leaving behind
fancy spider web capes.

Dust Fairies are cheerful,
devoted, and bright.
Each has a gift
that feels wonderfully right.

There was one exception
in this happy group.
And his sad, little soul
was beginning to droop.

While the others were dancing
and twirling about,
one fairy boy
sat alone with a pout.

Artie sat quietly,
his head in the clouds,
wondering how
he fit in with this crowd.

Flitting around in the dark,
was no thrill.
But, Artie possessed
a much different skill.

Instead of spending his nights
with the crew,
Artie had something
more pressing to do.

No one knew why,
and he didn't say.
But, night after night,
he went on his way.

He snatched lint from carpets,

and fur left by pets.

Stray hair, caught on brushes,
is what he liked best.

His fellow Dust Fairies,
they didn't much care,
for Artie's collection
of tidbits and hair.

He gathered his treasures,
and hid them from view,
in corners and shadows,
so nobody knew.

Scrounging and hoarding
brought Artie great joy.
But, deep down inside,
he was a sad fairy boy.

He needed a pal
to cuddle and hold.
A soft, little buddy
would lighten the load.

So on a cold night,
feeling lost and alone,
Artie created
a friend of his own.

He started with lint
and a tangle of hair,

and tucked whispers of fuzz
here and there.

When he was finished,
his heart swelled with pride.
At last, a companion
to stay by his side.

The Dust Bunny was perfect
from toes up to ears.

Its heavenly face,
brought Artie to tears.

Word spread quickly
about Artie's new chum.
And soon all the Dust Fairies
begged to have one.

Artie obliged
each and every request.
He worked, and he toiled,
and he gave it his best.

To this very day,
all fairies have one,
a lovely Dust Bunny,
to join in their fun!

Dust Bunnies are crafted
from lint, fuzz, and hair.
If you happen to find one,
treat it with care.

The fairy who lost it
will be worried sick,
and rush back to claim it
lickety-split.

So, the next time
your mother asks you to clean,
tell her The Legend,
explain what it means.

A neat, tidy room
may be the strict rule,
but removing the Dust Bunnies
is simply quite cruel.

The End

The Writer

Michelle Eastman began her career as an elementary teacher in the West Des Moines School District. At Iowa Public Television, she wrote educational content for teachers and students in over two-hundred Iowa school districts. When Michelle is not chasing dust bunnies, she likes to cuddle up with a good book and her son. She and her family live in Waukee, Iowa. Michelle is a proud supporter of the Animal Rescue League of Iowa.

Visit her at www.michelleeastmanbooks.com

The Illustrator

Kevin Richter has always drawn, doodled, painted and scribbled. He loves it so much that he makes a living doing it. He lives with his wife and their two sons in the beautiful English town of Royal Tunbridge Wells in Kent.

Visit Kev at www.kevtoon.com

Made in the USA
Las Vegas, NV
28 September 2021